D0998054

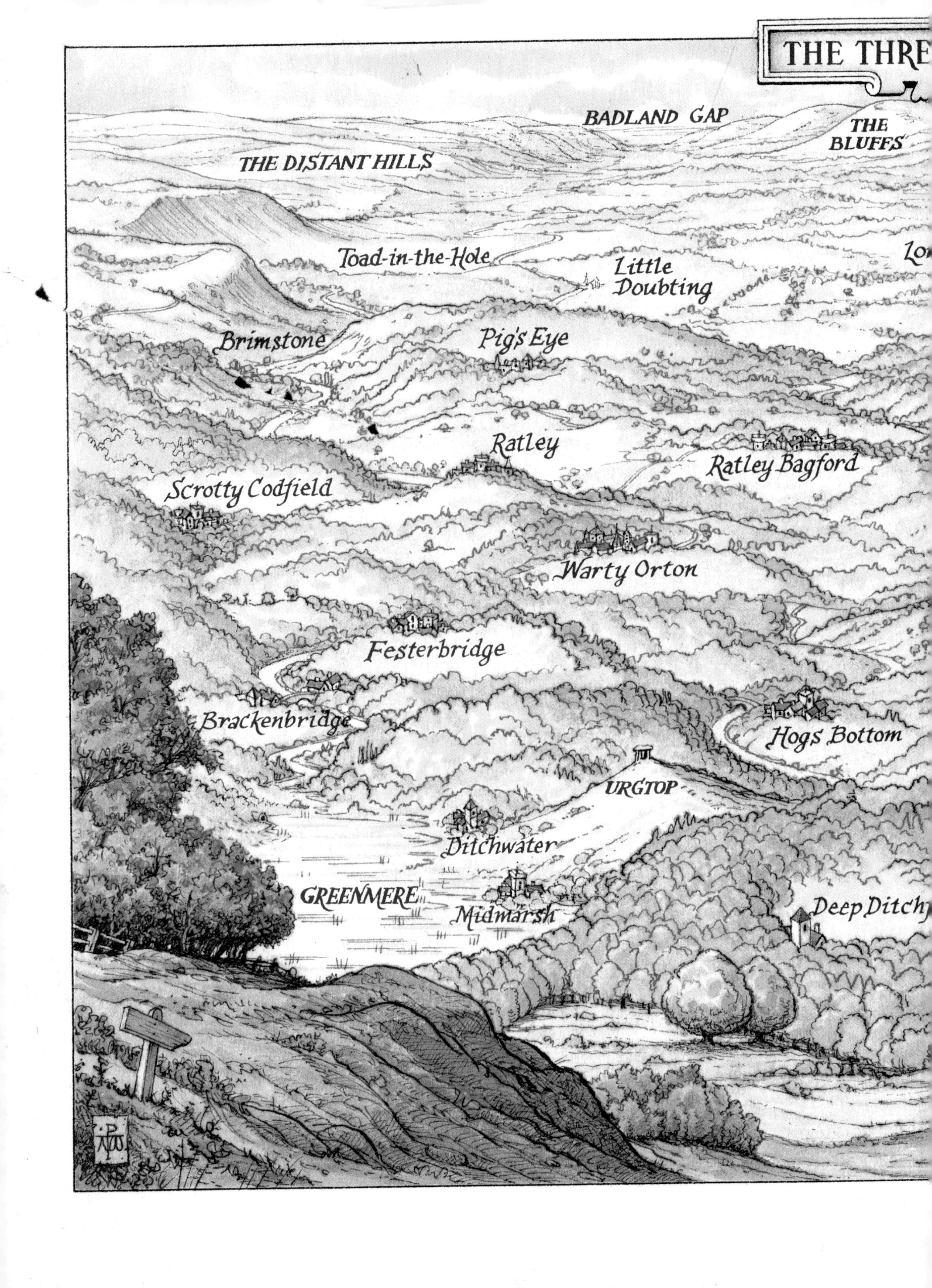
THE THRE
BADLAND GAP
THE BLUFFS
THE DISTANT HILLS
Toad-in-the-Hole
Little Doubting
Brimstone
Pig's Eye
Ratley
Ratley Bagford
Scrotty Codfield
Warty Orton
Festerbridge
Brackenbridge
Hogs Bottom
URGTOP
Ditchwater
GREENMERE
Midmarsh
Deep Ditch

COUNTIES
Cold Comfort
Pig's Norton
alding
THE BLASTED HEATH
Wormwood
EAST MOORS
Gibbards
BLACK LAGOON
HERMIT ISLAND
THE OLD FOREST
DARKLING
WOOD
Down-in-the-Dumps
Hobbs End
THE OLD MINE

THE ADVENTURES OF
MUFFIN PIGDOOM

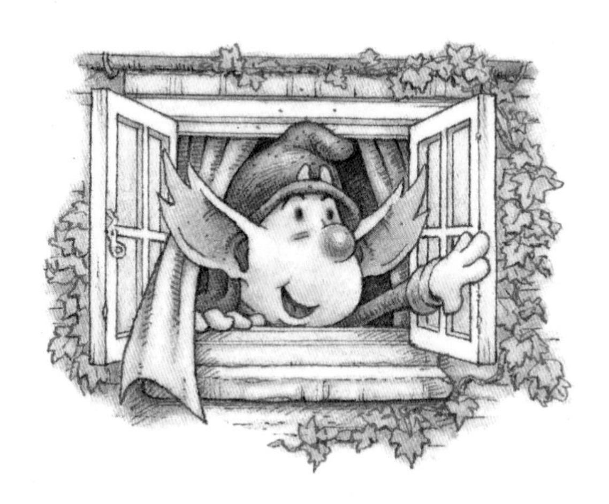

MUFFIN and the KEEPER

For Anita

First published in Great Britain 1996
by Heinemann Young Books
Published 1996 by Mammoth
an imprint of Reed Consumer Books Ltd.
Michelin House, 81 Fulham Road, London SW3 6RB
and Auckland, Melbourne, Singapore and Toronto

10 9 8 7 6 5 4 3 2 1

0 7497 2961 9

A CIP catalogue record for this title
is available from the British Library

Produced by Mandarin Offset Ltd
Printed and bound in China

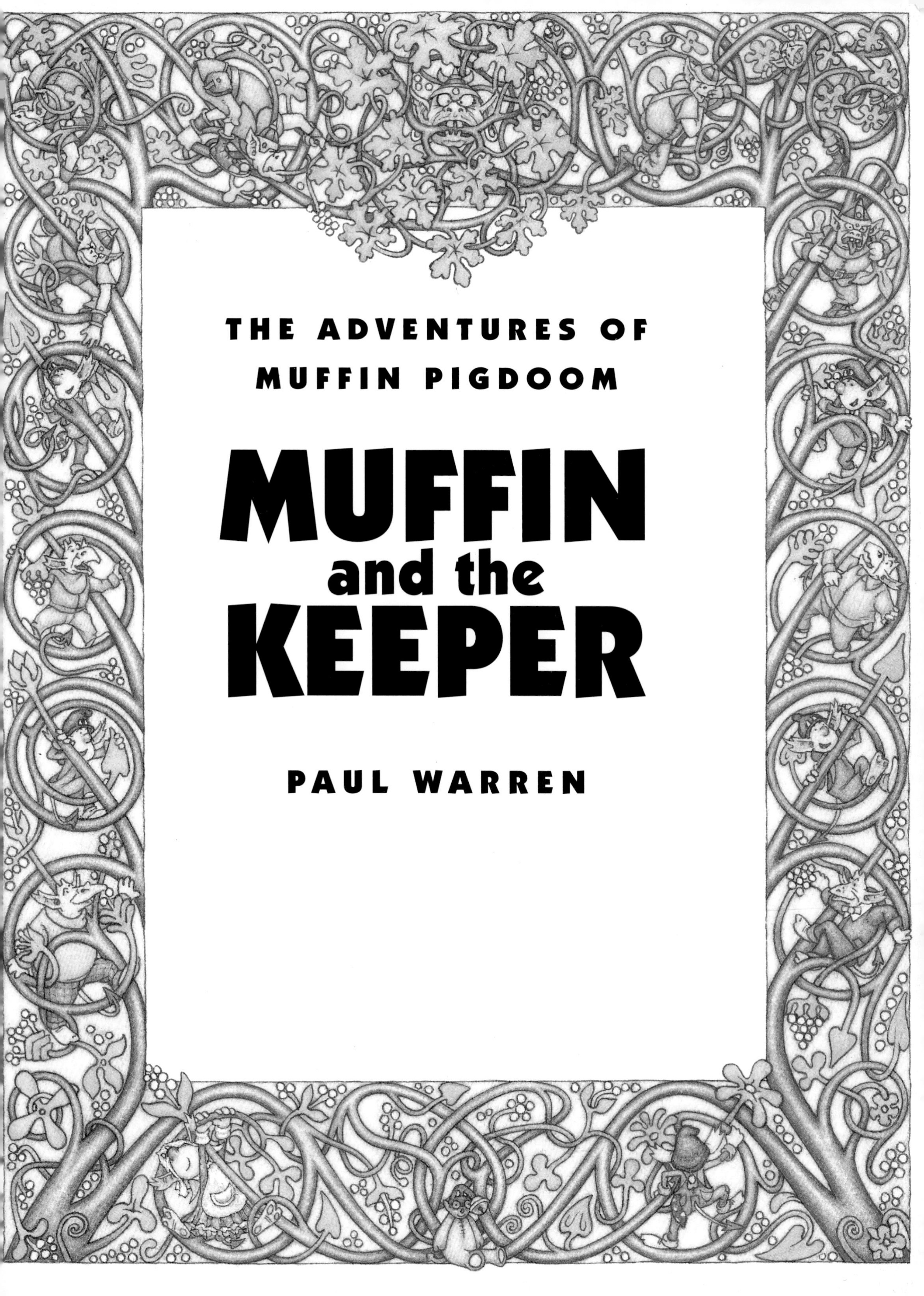

THE ADVENTURES OF MUFFIN PIGDOOM

MUFFIN and the KEEPER

PAUL WARREN

Muffin Pigdoom was up at daybreak.

"Come on," he called as he tumbled out of bed and ran round the house. "It's a lovely morning!"

"Go away," grumbled his sister, Camilla.

"It's too early," Muffin's brother, Festus, complained.
Muffin's parents pulled the covers closer, but his Uncle Carbuncle stretched and got up.
"All right, Muffin," he said sleepily. "Breakfast time."

After breakfast the spring cleaning began. Muffin was keen to join in, but sometimes he got in the way.

"Let me help," he said, standing on his father's tail.

Just then there was a loud knocking at the front door. Uncle Carbuncle looked anxious.

"That sounds like the Urgs," he said.

The front door flew open and in burst the Urgs. They made a frightful row until one ugly brute, bigger than the rest, stepped forward.

"Silence!" he shouted. "I'm Captain Scumbag. I'm here to collect your Spring Tax. Pay up or you'll go to the Assizes!"

Muffin turned pale. He'd heard that people who went to the Assizes were sent away for years.

His father protested angrily. "We can't afford your Spring Tax. This purse contains all we have in the world."

Captain Scumbag snatched the purse away. "This will do nicely," he growled. "Fetch the Keeper!"

At that a wild-looking fellow with a sack emerged from the crowd and sang in a harsh, croaking voice:

Studs the Goblin picks his nose,
With his bag he comes and goes
He's not worried if you're sad –
But lack of gold makes him mad!

With long bony fingers the Keeper grabbed the purse and thrust it into his sack.

"Let that be a lesson to you," Captain Scumbag said sternly, and with that he turned and led his troop out of the house and up the road to Ratley Bagford.

Although Muffin was frightened, the sight of the Keeper's sack also made him very cross. Those Urgs were so nasty, so greedy. Before his parents could stop him, he slipped out of the door and ran after them.

The Urgs went quickly on their long bent legs, and soon Muffin was left far behind. He paused to catch his breath.

"Hello, Muffin."

"Pustule! What are you doing?"

His friend peeped out from behind the hedgerow.

"Hiding!" he whispered. "Urgs went by, lots of them."

One went over the heath towards Hobbs End – a nasty-looking creature with a sack!"

"The Keeper!" cried Muffin. "That's the one I'm after."

Muffin ran and ran, and soon he found himself on the edge of Darkling Wood. This was a scary place and his mother had warned him about it many times but today he ran on without stopping.

He had not gone far when he heard strange sounds close by. Stepping carefully, he crept up to a large tree and peered round the trunk.

He opened his eyes wide.

There was the Keeper, down on all fours, scratching at a hole in the ground.

He unearthed a small box, and his yellow eyes rolled with delight. “Gold!” he cackled as he emptied the box into his sack.

Muffin watched closely for amongst the shining coins he could see his father’s purse. He’s robbed *lots* of people! he thought.

At last the Keeper got up. He threw the sack over his shoulder and with a terrible laugh strode into the wood.

The trees pressed in closely as Muffin struggled after him. Tangled roots and branches plucked at his arms and legs, and it was hard going. I wonder where I am? he thought.

Suddenly the Keeper stopped.

What was it?

Muffin hid behind a bush and his heart skipped a beat for ahead was a clearing, and in the clearing was a warty old thunder-lizard, as big as a house.

Muffin had never seen such a thing before, and he wondered what it ate for breakfast.

Luckily, the thunder-lizard was fast asleep.

Suddenly a voice hissed, "Don't move!" Then two friendly faces peered cautiously from the leaves.

"Fergus and Fungus!" said Muffin. "What are you doing?"

"We didn't mean to startle you," whispered Fergus. "But we've just seen an Urg go by."

"That's the Keeper," said Muffin grimly. "He's stolen my Dad's purse. I'm following him."

"We need a plan to catch that Urg," said Fergus.

"There's a blocked off tunnel with an iron gate at the Old Mine," said Fungus. "It's perfect for a trap!"

"How do we get him there?" Muffin asked doubtfully.

"What if I make noises like a wounded animal?" said Fergus. "He's sure to follow. He won't miss the chance of a free meal."

"That's it!" cried Muffin. "Come on!"

"But quietly past the thunder-lizard," said Fungus. "I'd hate to be the one who wakes *him* up."

They tiptoed through the clearing,
and heard the Keeper grunting and puffing ahead.

"He's slowing up," said Fergus. "Now's our chance."

He ran on and Muffin and Fungus crept quietly from the path. Now the trees began to thin, and soon they emerged to see the mouth of a cave yawning in a rocky hillside.

"Be careful," warned Fungus. "There are lots of deep holes around here. If you fall in one, you'll be lost forever."

Muffin pricked up his ears. He could hear noises in the forest now: howling and the sound of a sack being shaken.

Fungus hissed, "Run for the gate! You look for a stone. When the Urg's inside we'll jam it shut!"

Muffin and Fungus separated, and a moment later Fergus burst from the trees and raced towards the cave. Behind him came the Keeper – *crash!* – charging up the hill.

"What have we here?" he said in a hideous voice as he stepped into the cave. "Something for the pot?"

Immediately Fungus sprang up. "Quick, Fergus! Run! He's in the trap! Push! *Heave!*"

But the gate would not budge. It was old and the hinges were rusty.

"A fine trap this is," laughed the Keeper, grabbing hold of the twins. "All you've caught is yourselves!"

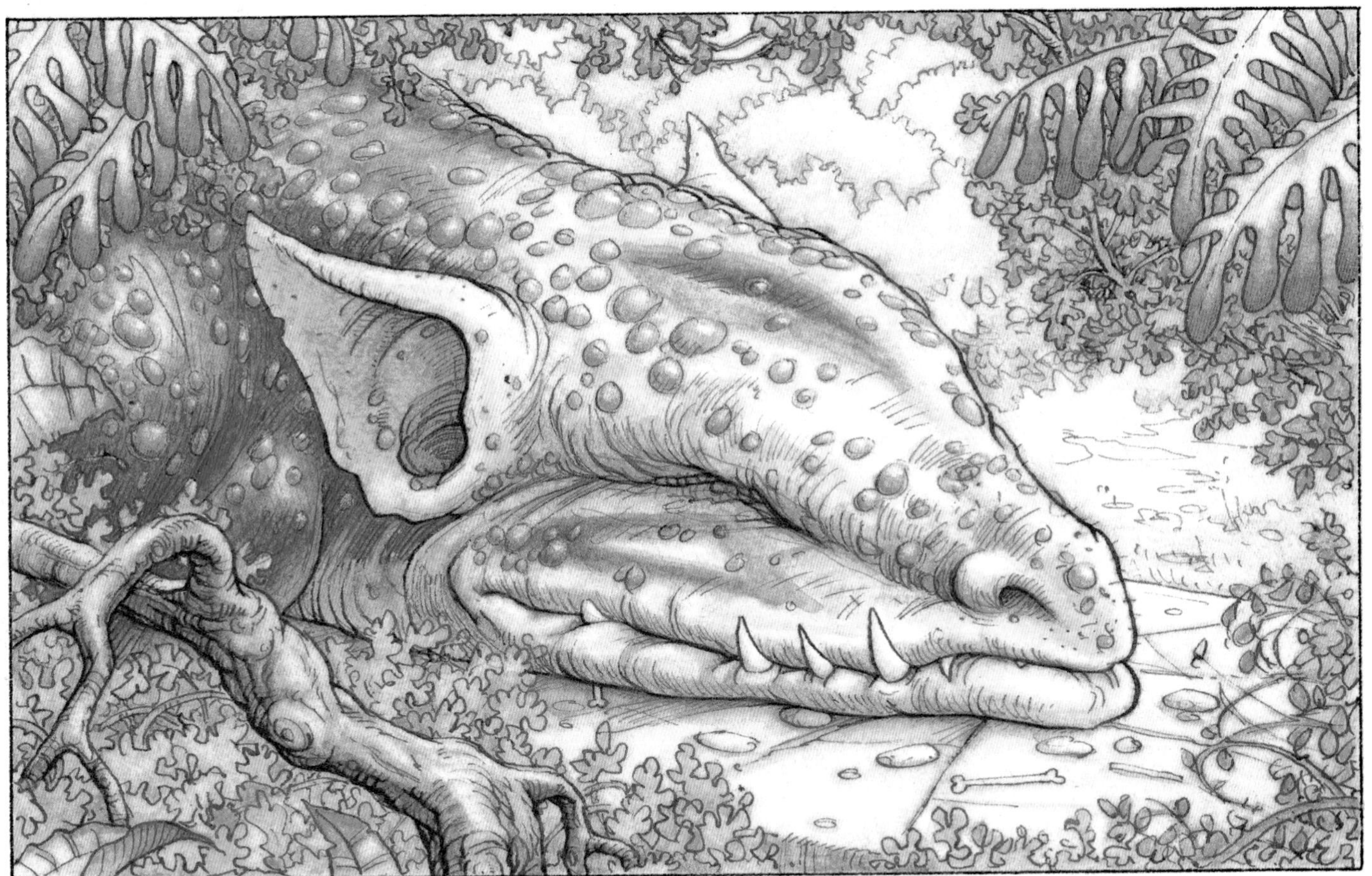

From his hiding place, Muffin watched, aghast. What could he do to save his friends!

Quickly, he turned and ran like the wind to the clearing where the thunder-lizard slept.

"Wake up! Wake up!" he shouted.
The monster grunted and raised its head. "Can't catch me!" shouted Muffin. He crossed his eyes and stuck his tongue out. I hope this trick works, he thought, then ran for dear life.

Meanwhile, the Keeper was dangling Fergus and Fungus over the edge of a deep hole.

"You'll rue the day you tangled with me," he jeered.

Suddenly he heard shouts and saw Muffin running from the wood, straight towards him.

"Bless my boots," he laughed. "If it isn't another one."

But his smile soon vanished when he saw the thunder-lizard crashing through the trees behind him.

Filled with panic, he dived into the hole. The twins ran with Muffin into the cave.

Finding no bones to crunch, the thunder-lizard crashed angrily back into the wood.

They waited until everything was quiet and then nervously emerged from the cave.

"Look there," hissed Muffin, pointing to the hole. "Can you see what I can see?"

Down below, the Keeper clung desperately to a root.

"Give us a hand," he shouted.

"I want my Dad's money back first," said Muffin.

The Keeper's yellow eyes flashed. "Take it," he said.

Muffin reached into the hole. He untied the neck of the sack and withdrew his father's purse.

"Now give us a hand," demanded the Keeper.

"I can't help you and that great sack," said Muffin. "You'll have to pass it up first."

"Never," growled the Keeper, and he shook with rage. "It's mine, all mine!"

"Quickly," said Muffin. "That root won't hold forever."

But the Keeper didn't answer. The root creaked, there was a loud *crack!* and he was gone.

"Silly creature," said Muffin. "But at least he didn't get this." He shook the purse triumphantly and smiled and thanked his friends. When it was time to go home, Fergus and Fungus went with Muffin to the crossroads at Deep Ditchford. To avoid the wood, he took the long way back.

It was dusk when Muffin came racing over the heath to Pigdoom Cottage.

"We thought you'd gone for good!" cried Mrs Pigdoom as he ran into her arms.

Muffin smiled and showed them his father's purse.

"I've had such an adventure!" he told them.

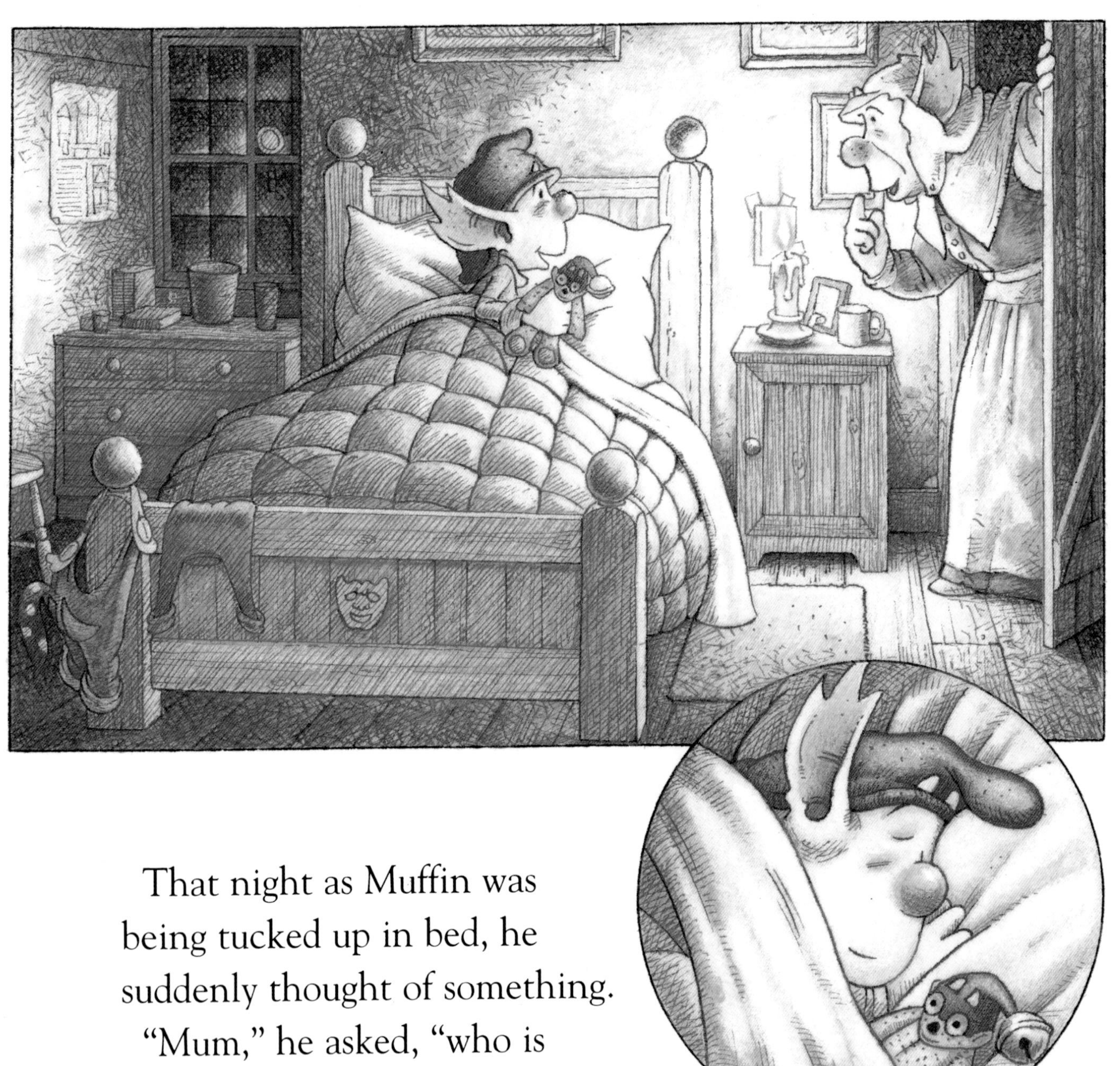

That night as Muffin was being tucked up in bed, he suddenly thought of something.

"Mum," he asked, "who is Studs the Goblin?"

Mrs Pigdoom had forgotten the Keeper's strange song.

"A friend of Captain Scumbag's, I shouldn't wonder."

She chuckled and kissed him on the nose. "Whatever will you think of next?"

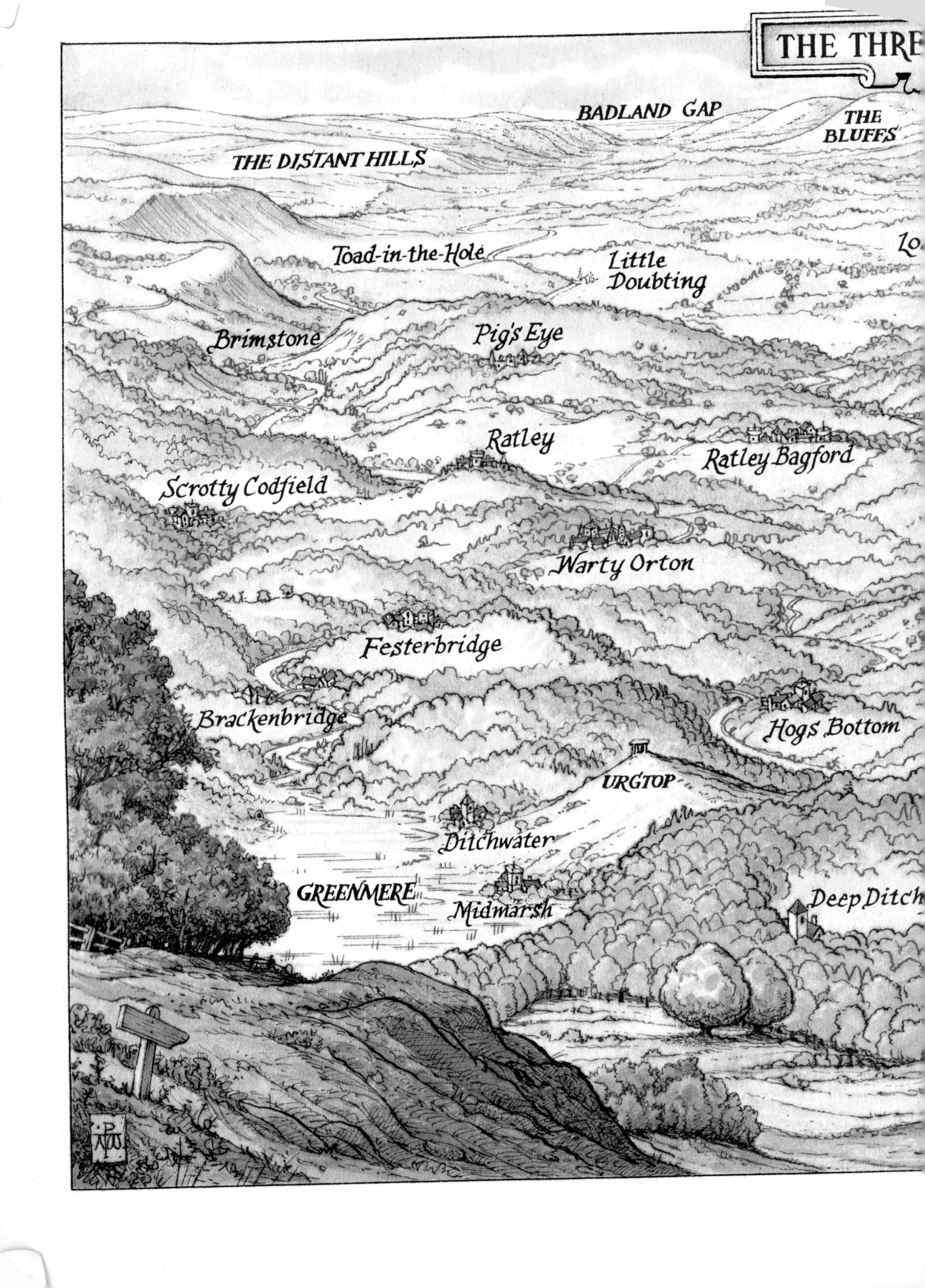
THE THRE
BADLAND GAP
THE BLUFFS
THE DISTANT HILLS
Toad-in-the-Hole
Little Doubting
Brimstone
Pig's Eye
Ratley
Ratley Bagford
Scrotty Codfield
Warty Orton
Festerbridge
Brackenbridge
Hogs Bottom
URGTOP
Ditchwater
GREENMERE
Midmarsh
Deep Ditch

OUNTIES
Cold Comfort
Pig's Norton
alding
Wormwood
THE BLASTED HEATH
EAST MOORS
Gibbards
BLACK LAGOON
HERMIT ISLAND
THE OLD FOREST
DARKLING
WOOD
Down-in-the-Dumps
Hobbs End
THE OLD MINE